PR
THE

★★★★★

"A fantastic beast of a story!"
– Steve Stred (via Amazon)

★★★★★

"Follow the strange men to the basement and see what Joe Koch has created."
- Hailey P. (via Amazon)

DEMAIN PUBLISHING

Short Sharp Shocks!

Book 0: Dirty Paws - Dean M. Drinkel
Book 1: Patient K - Barbie Wilde
Book 2: The Stranger & The Ribbon – Tim Dry
Book 3: Asylum Of Shadows – Stephanie Ellis
Book 4: Monster Beach – Ritchie Valentine Smith
Book 5: Beasties & Other Stories – Martin Richmond
Book 6: Every Moon Atrocious – Emile-Louis Tomas Jouvet
Book 7: A Monster Met – Liz Tuckwell
Book 8: The Intruders & Other Stories – Jason D. Brawn
Book 9: The Other – David Youngquist
Book 10: Symphony Of Blood – Leah Crowley
Book 11: Shattered – Anthony Watson
Book 12: The Devil's Portion – Benedict J. Jones
Book 13: Cinders Of A Blind Man Who Could See – Kev Harrison
Book 14: Dulce Et Decorum Est – Dan Howarth
Book 15: Blood, Bears & Dolls – Allison Weir
Book 16: The Forest Is Hungry – Chris Stanley
Book 17: The Town That Feared Dusk – Calvin Demmer
Book 18: Night Of The Rider – Alyson Faye
Book 19: Isidora's Pawn – Erik Hofstatter
Book 20: Plain – D.T. Griffith
Book 21: Supermassive Black Mass – Matthew Davis
Book 22: Whispers Of The Sea (& Other Stories) – L. R. Bonehill
Book 23: Magic – Eric Nash
Book 24: The Plague – R.J. Meldrum
Book 25: Candy Corn – Kevin M. Folliard

Book 26: The Elixir – Lee Allen Howard
Book 27: Breaking The Habit – Yolanda Sfetsos
Book 28: Forfeit Tissue – C. C. Adams
Book 29: Crown Of Thorns – Trevor Kennedy
Book 30: The Encampment / Blood Memory – Zachary Ashford
Book 31: Dreams Of Lake Drukka / Exhumation – Mike Thorn
Book 32: Apples / Snail Trails – Russell Smeaton
Book 33: An Invitation To Darkness – Hailey Piper
Book 34: The Necessary Evils & Sick Girl – Dan Weatherer
Book 35: The Couvade – Joe Koch
Book 36: The Camp Creeper & Other Stories – Dave Jeffery
Book 37: Flaying Sins – Ian Woodhead
Book 38: Hearts & Bones – Theresa Derwin
Book 39: The Unbeliever & The Intruder – Morgan K. Tanner
Book 40: The Coffin Walk – Richard Farren Barber
Book 41: The Straitjacket In The Woods – Kitty R. Kane
Book 42: Heart Of Stone – M. Brandon Robbins
Book 43: Bits – R.A. Busby
Book 44: Last Meal In Osaka & Other Stories – Gary Buller
Book 45: The One That Knows No Fear – Steve Stred
Book 46: The Birthday Girl & Other Stories – Christopher Beck
Book 47: Crowded House & Other Stories - S.J. Budd
Book 48: Hand To Mouth – Deborah Sheldon
Book 49: Moonlight Gunshot Mallet Flame / A Little Death – Alicia Hilton
Book 50: Dark Corners - David Charlesworth

Murder! Mystery! Mayhem!
Maggie Of My Heart – Alyson Faye
The Funeral Birds – Paula R.C. Readman
Cursed – Paul M. Feeney

Anthologies
The Darkest Battlefield – Tales Of WW1/Horror

Horror Novellas
House Of Wrax – Raven Dane
A Quiet Apocalypse – Dave Jeffery

General Fiction
Joe – Terry Grimwood
Finding Jericho – Dave Jeffery

THE COUVADE
BY
JOE KOCH

A SHORT SHARP SHOCKS! BOOK

BOOK 35

© Demain 2019 / 2020

COPYRIGHT INFORMATION

Entire contents copyright © 2019 / 2020 Joe Koch / Demain Publishing

Cover © 2020 Adrian Baldwin

First Published 2019

All rights reserved. No part of this publication may be reproduced, stored or transmitted in any form or by any means, electronic, mechanical, photocopying, recording, scanning or otherwise without written permission from the publisher. It is illegal to copy this book, post it to a website or distribute it by any other means without permission.

What follows is entirely a work of fiction. The names, characters and incidents portrayed in it are the work of the author's imagination. Any resemblance to actual persons, living or dead, events or localities is entirely co-incidental.

Joe Koch asserts the moral right to be identified as the author of this work in its totality.

Designations used by companies to distinguish their products are often claimed as trademarks. All brand names and product names used in this book and on its cover are trade names, service marks, trademarks and registered trademarks of their respective owners. The publishers and the book are not associated with any product or vendor mentioned in this book. None of the companies within the book have endorsed the book.

For further information, please visit:

WEB: www.demainpublishing.com
TWITTER: @DemainPubUk
FACEBOOK: Demain Publishing
INSTAGRAM: demainpublishing

CONTENTS

THE COUVADE 9
BIOGRAPHY 47
ADRIAN BALDWIN (COVER ARTIST) 48
DEMAIN PUBLISHING 51

THE COUVADE

Martin finessed the old lock until he felt the tumblers align and slide. He hesitated before entering. The baroque wolf-head door knocker seemed to sniff him. Steam billowed from its forged-iron nose, mixing with Martin's own cold breath. Martin froze. He could swear he heard a huffing sound. His thighs tensed, ready to bolt, and then he realized the noise was only Jerome shoving snow off the box buried next to the steps.

Jerome kicked away the snow. "The postmark on this box says December tenth. Merry freaking Christmas."

Martin made himself breathe again, and opened the old oak door with well-practiced composure. "Surely we can salvage a decent meal or two from the remains."

Jerome hoisted the soggy Haute Fresh box out of the snow and shifted it onto his knee to get a better grip. The cardboard bottom collapsed. Jerome's socks were already soaked, and now his best Johnson and Murphy casuals were covered with a week's worth of shrink-wrapped chicken and flaccid kale. Jerome dropped the whole mess down the steps and flung the useless box across the garden bed to vent his frustration. Martin ducked inside and switched on a light.

Jerome stomped in behind, yanked off his shoes and clapped the soles together. Snow chunks flew. Martin slid out of his insulated boots and went down the hall to find an old towel in the linen closet.

Amazing how nothing had changed, except the house looked smaller than Martin remembered. The familiar scent of pine cleaner pervaded the closet. On the exact shelf where Martin's uncle had always kept the cleaning supplies, rags were folded and stacked next to bottles arranged with military precision. Uncle Michel's rags were the quality of an average home's bath towels, and Martin knew if he measured the space between each bottle of cleaner, he'd find it correct within a sixteenth of an inch.

Swiping a shoe from Jerome, Martin dabbed the leather dry. He gave special attention to seams and stitches where moisture might hide and corrode with time. Jerome slumped against the wall, the other shoe drooping in his hand.

"What about dinner?"

"The town market's not far." Martin finished detailing and placed the clean shoe near the heat register. He pulled the second shoe away and started work while Jerome pouted. "Or we can eat out."

"Oh God. No more driving. I'll die."

"Perhaps we can find something delicious for you in Uncle Michel's larder."

"Like what? Pickled turnips from the nineteen eighties?"

"No," Martin said. "Pickled eyeballs from the sixteenth century. Witch's eyeballs."

"Don't talk to me like a fifth-grader."

"Then stop acting like one. You're not going to starve." Martin finished tending the soiled shoe, aligned it with its mate, and knelt. He spoke to the floor while he rearranged the rescued pair. "You should get out of those wet socks."

Jerome put his hands on Martin's shoulders. Martin tensed. Jerome waited for the subtle shift in Martin's breathing and demeanor that signaled it was okay to be close. He noticed Martin's trapezius muscles were more strained and tight than usual. Jerome pressed into the stiff spots and felt Martin lean into him rather than pull away, so he pressed harder, reshaping, smoothing away the knots. Martin closed his eyes and let his head drop back.

Jerome struggled with putting what he wanted to ask Martin into words. He settled for something general. "So how are you doing with everything, like for real?"

"Terrible."

Martin's voice leaked bitterness. The phone call from the bank handling his uncle's trust had been a shock. How was it possible for Martin to be the sole surviving heir to Uncle Michel's estate? Martin argued with the bank that he'd been estranged for over twenty years. It was not his responsibility. Not his family.

After he calmed down and accepted the situation, Martin did the reasonable things: met with an attorney and accountant, and planned the extended holiday trip to make a decision about the house. He also did unreasonable things. He snapped at Jerome with increasing intolerance, berated him for the smallest misstep.

As a psychiatrist, Martin understood the chemical science behind emotions. He made his living curing passions and managing their undesirable effects. He knew the standard treatment techniques, what prescriptions to write. But he knew no way to name the changes erupting inside of him without passing his darkness on to Jerome.

Cousin Bobby had been a bully. That much Martin would admit. To speak more risked ruining everything.

Martin looked up at Jerome's relaxed smile and comforting heft. "I don't know how I'd do this without you. I shouldn't put you through any of it. If you need a break, I understand."

"I'm not going anywhere. Do you think you can scare me away? Go ahead, do your best."

"I don't deserve you."

"Nobody does," Jerome said. "I'm basically a gay saint. So, anyway, tell me how we handle dinner out here. I need to learn about this country lifestyle. Am I supposed to chase down a rabbit in the woods? Catch it with my bare hands? Or can we maybe order Chinese?"

"That seems terribly rude after the blizzard. Stay put and warm up. I'll go back to town and pick something up."

"Don't you know drivers live for snow? We'll tip double. And a spooky house out in the boonies bumps up the mileage. They'll be thrilled." Jerome scrolled and dialed, overriding Martin's concern. "You know, I worked for Gourmet Dash in Philly. We fought for the calls when it was bad weather."

"I imagine you won every time. With your charming personality, of course."

"You know it. Hi, we'd like to place an order. Let me check. Hey, is the address here 1521 Dolphin?"

"Dauphine," Martin corrected, stressing the last syllable.

"Yep: 1521 Dolphin. Hello? Damn, I'm on hold."

"Please. There's no need for cursing."

"Oh babe, I'm sorry." Then Jerome spoke into the phone. "Uh-huh. Yeah, we're the family. Jerome Verdun. Here with my husband, Martin Verdun. We just got in and look, we're kind of starved, so can we get that order rolling?" Jerome shook his head and mouthed *here we go again*.

Martin marveled at Jerome's easy honesty. No secrets, no shame. After hanging up, Jerome gave Martin's shoulder a squeeze. "Hey, you're okay with being out in your hometown, right? I mean, it's what we talked about."

"Absolutely. We agreed. Nothing changes here."

"Solid. Stuck in that car all day." Jerome stretched. "Damn, I wish we had some beer. I mean darn. That's three strikes, isn't it?"

"You're forgiven. You've earned leniency for putting up with me lately. Beer and cheap food sounds blissfully mundane, a perfect contrast to the surreal prospect of a night in this house." *But I'm not a child*, Martin thought, *and all of them are dead.*

Dead and buried, underground. Unless...

"Why don't I fetch a bottle of wine from uncle's cellar? It isn't beer, but you might be surprised. Will that do?"

Jerome didn't answer right away. Martin's light tone caught him off guard. "It's no big thing. I'm good."

"Did I ever tell you Uncle Michel's collection was featured in a Parisian journal? Imagine: an American cellar lauded as one of the best in its day. I can't wait to see what's left of it. I remember what seemed like hundreds of bottles, miles of racks. Of course, I was a child then. Memory is such a trickster. Now that it occurs to me, I believe we must go to the cellar immediately."

Jerome blocked him. "Hold up. Weren't we supposed to talk about this first? You were pretty serious about last night."

"It's my professional opinion that the talking cure is a myth. The cellar is very large, quite frightening to a young child. Nothing adults need to talk about."

"Well, how about I grab a bottle and you chill up here? Someone's got to get the door when the food comes. There's no telling what I'll start gnawing on if you don't feed me soon. The claw foot on that fancy chair is starting to look mighty tasty."

"I'll make certain we feed you well enough tonight, my love. Don't worry; we'll hear that monstrosity on the door rattling for miles. I'm perfectly fine, and you don't know wine. Come now." The manic gleam in Martin's eyes told Jerome the debate was over.

Descending into the cellar, Martin didn't expect the memories to hit him so hard. He aged backwards with every step. He wanted to turn back, but felt too small and helpless to make a choice.

Martin's sense of smell went wild. The woody aroma of smoke lingered in the lime plaster. Uncle Michel had stoked an oven deep in the farthest cove to prevent the rising damp that tainted corks and oxygenated fine vintages into vinegar. The scent of burning dust, a fragrance like incense and old books, lingered at the edges of the rough walls. The porous nature of the stone on the floor echoed with a metallic scent. Martin's memories rang like warning bells. Deeper in the earth where the floors became dirt, ancient dried rafters held back childhood fears too pungent for Martin to name.

Jerome turned in a slow circle at the base of the stone staircase, gawking, taking in the spider-leg radius of tunnels. "Man, you weren't kidding. Looks like this place covers more ground than the whole house."

"Yes. The caverns were here first, long before construction of the dwelling place."

"It's like a maze."

Martin crouched with his back to the wall. He kept his voice down to reduce echoes. "A good place to play hide and seek. Once, this was a catacomb. The clan kept their forbearers close."

"Fucking cool. Are people buried here?" Jerome filled the space with his broad voice and easy swagger. He wandered through the racks with impunity while Martin kept vigilant watch. Distracted by the horror movie aesthetic, Jerome didn't catch Martin's eyes darting from side to side. He didn't notice how Martin poised near the ground as still as an animal ready to flee or pounce.

Bobby's here, Martin thought, afraid to move, afraid to blink.

He was sure of it. The sun rose and set every day, the moon waxed and waned each cycle, and Bobby was here, waiting for him as he'd promised. He'd forced Martin to promise, petting his smaller cousin, more threat than comfort. *Good boy*, Bobby said. *Now say it again. Three times makes it a pact.*

Bang, bang, bang.

The door knocker rang like three silver bullets shot in the dark, an invisible quarry silenced, efficacy unknown. Martin sprang from his haunches, bolted up the stairs, ran through the kitchen, hallway, and past the great room. He flung open the foyer door fueled on a mad instinct to keep running and almost plowed over a small person on the porch.

The outdoor lamp hung at an odd angle, casting light down the steps instead of illuminating the porch. The small person presented Martin with a plain white pastry box. The figure appeared faceless, cloaked in shadow. Martin unfolded bills from his wallet and held them out. The shrouded enigma raised its hand in refusal. Its palm was whiter than the glare of snow on the surrounding gardens, as luminous as the full moon shining overhead after the night's violent storm. Martin felt stupid and blinded. He stared at the undersides of silver rings banding the slender fingers. Their unseen insignia beguiled him. Martin imagined they held clues to the creature's identity.

Martin realized he must accept or refuse the box. He shook off his idiot fascination, took the pastry box, and pushed the bills forward again. "Please, for your trouble. This weather."

Something in the figure before him suggested teeth. The small person shook their head and backed away. Martin heard the chiming of bells as they receded into the darkness. He felt like he was dreaming. *This house*, Martin thought, *it's making me disassociate.* "Thank you," he said, although the silent visitor had vanished.

"They didn't take my tip." Martin put the pastry box on the counter. It seemed too lightweight for such a large container. "How much did you put on the card?"

"Huh? I have cash. Do you need some?" Jerome rummaged in the kitchen, disorganizing drawers and misplacing utensils. Cabinet doors hung open. "Where's the corkscrew?"

Martin felt pleased at the thought of Uncle Michel spinning in his grave as Jerome's sweet carelessness upended his household. The Verdun reign of terror overthrown, Martin replaced the ridiculous port glasses Jerome had chosen with the correct crystal without the urge to make a snide remark.

"Here. Let me take care of that."

Jerome grabbed something from the pastry box and crammed it into his mouth. Ignoring Martin's fastidiousness about manners, Jerome spoke while he chewed. "Oh thank god. I was ready to die. How'd I do?"

Martin sniffed the cork, avoiding the sight of Jerome's packed jaw. He heard it working up and down. "Very good. Of course, a Burgundy rather outclasses the meal."

"Where's the rest of it?"

"What?"

"The food. There's nothing here but a ton of dried out bread rolls."

Bang, bang, bang.

The massive cast iron door-knocker boomed.

"I guess that's it."

A teenager in a lumpy down jacket and red uniform shirt waited on the doorstep. He wore a nametag that said Todd. He nodded as a greeting and pulled three take-out boxes with dragon designs on them out of an insulated carrier. He waited while Martin looked at him, baffled.

"Uh, how's it going?"

"Oh no," Martin said. "There must have been a mistake."

Jerome came to the rescue and took the boxes. He handed Todd a wad of cash. "Keep the change. The roads are crazy tonight."

Todd grinned at the money and then at Jerome. "Thanks, man."

Martin frowned past Todd at the car idling in the driveway. The noise, lights and exhaust made Martin wonder how the previous visitor had appeared and vanished with no visible transportation. He'd heard no sound except the chiming of bells. Todd glanced back at his car. "Sorry about that. Best to leave her running when it's this cold out." He looked at Martin and cleared his throat. "Excuse me, Mr Verdun?"

"Doctor," Martin corrected. "I'm so sorry, have we met before?"

"No, uh, doctor, but everyone around here knows about the Verduns. No offense, you all kinda look alike. So, I was wondering, do you need any help out here? Cleaning up?"

The Haute Fresh box and contents still splayed across the garden bed as though ravaged by animals. Martin was mortified. "No. Not at all. We're fine."

Jerome intervened again. "Wait up, that's not a bad idea. The basement's huge.

Why don't you come by tomorrow. I bet we can find some work for you."

"Yes, sir. I can do that. Thank you!"

"No problem. Drive safe out there."

Todd's car flooded the driveway with noise and smoke as he pulled out, still grinning. Martin shook his head at Jerome. "What are you thinking? We don't know anything about him."

Jerome shrugged and dumped the take-out boxes on the table, spilling very little sauce. "He seemed like a nice kid. Needs the money, I bet. You never had to drive an old beater like that, did you?"

Martin gathered plates, napkins and silverware from the kitchen. He arranged two tidy place settings and decanted two glasses of wine. He handed one to Jerome. Then he remembered the plain white pastry box in the kitchen. Dry or not, it might be a nice touch to plate up dinner rolls. Martin pulled a platter from a cupboard and opened the box.

It was empty.

"Where did they go?"

"Where food's supposed to go," said Jerome. "In my belly."

"You ate all the rolls in the box?"

"I was hungry."

"How many were there?"

"Not that many. It wasn't really full."

"You said it was a ton, if I recall."

"Well, they were good, in a weird way. I couldn't stop."

"You're a monster. Don't blame me when you get sick. How did you even have time? Perhaps you might have considered sharing instead of stuffing yourself."

"You wouldn't have liked them anyway. Speaking of stuffing myself, why don't we sit down and eat. I'm ready for some protein. This wine is really great."

Later, Martin washed the dishes and scolded Jerome. "Eating like that will catch up with you eventually, no matter how much you work out. I'm only concerned for your health. I don't care if you get fat. I do care if you have a heart attack."

Jerome didn't mind Martin's nagging. The right amount of criticism said someone cared about him, and that hadn't always been the case.

"What can I say, babe? I'm a bottomless pit when I'm hungry. Or horny." Jerome stood behind Martin at the sink, put his arms around him, and nuzzled his ear. "The better to swallow you with, my dear."

"Don't be crass."

Jerome detected warmth in Martin's voice. He kept on being crass until he got Martin to give him what he was after.

***

Martin held back. His touch had an element missing. A new lover might mistake Martin's tentative pressure for reluctance, but Jerome knew Martin's body and knew how to provoke him. *Push me.* Jerome pushed Martin, not too hard, and challenged him to push back. Martin mirrored Jerome and gave a nervous laugh. *Come on. You can do better than that.* Martin shoved Jerome away. Jerome caught him mid-fall and they grappled. Martin's blood pumped harder with the aggressive instincts buried in his muscles and veins, hidden like a dirty secret. Jerome was ready to be overwhelmed and owned. He wanted all of Martin's rage.

He was strong enough to hold it.

Martin drove into Jerome and fought the images invading his head. Jerome demanded more, kept goading Martin to take power. *Do it, fuck me, harder.* Something in Martin's mind snapped into place. He occupied his body and the other body beneath him. He filled it, and when it gave in to him, he filled it more. That's what it kept begging for.

The words warped into cries that might have been pain or pleasure. It didn't matter which, because Martin was in control. Martin was the master and Bobby had no power to hurt him. Bobby was dead. All of them were dead. Dead bones, cellared and catacombed beneath the house, gaping mouths to defile, empty eye sockets to fuck. Martin would fuck all of them, everything, anything, and there was no one left alive to stop him.

Dead, dead, dead. The song echoed in his mind after his body had emptied itself of violence. The words were like bells, ringing, ringing.

Jerome didn't ask about the tears. He held Martin in his arms. *That was awesome. I love it when you can't stop.*

Reassurances lost on Martin, hiding his sick inner catacomb, protecting Jerome with his silence. Grateful his display of regret went unquestioned so that the past and everything unspeakable inside Martin remained buried, unexamined, and dead.

Martin wondered if Jerome was better off without him.

But I'm too selfish to let him go, Martin thought. The other thought, long forbidden, that he had no way to justify his wrong existence; he'd worked on putting behind him years ago. The impulse bobbed below the surface of his tears, a buoy that marked a dark escape route. Martin turned away.

Sleep refused to soothe Martin as Jerome drifted off, drugged with endorphin contentment. In Martin's half-waking dreams, the secrets of the house gathered around the bed while Jerome slept beside him. They ganged up to taunt. The Verdun family madness clung to Martin like someone else's skin: thick, tenacious, and vile. He endured hours wrapped in the skin and mated with a monstrous, mutating form. He spent whole days and weeks quaking in childish fear, anticipating the next brutal attack. The skin was forced on him. He must wear it to survive. *Say it,* Bobby's voice urged, hot in Martin's ear. *Three times makes it a pact.*

Martin leapt out of bed. He had to do something fast, drown his dreams in a river of action. He needed to escape the cage of the house, imagined running, running, deep into the forest, the way he ran wild as a boy, but this time, never coming back. No, no, he had a good life. He was a doctor, a responsible adult. All Martin had to endure was a few more weeks here, and then he'd sell the wretched place and forget the house existed. He'd leave his memories behind to molder within its ancient hull.

Sounds and scents dogged him from his dreams. A snow-laden branch scraped the window. Claws eager to claim him, grab him by the scruff. He had to get out. Tomorrow he'd be normal. Not now. Run.

The mess on the steps; Jerome wouldn't hear him outside. Good enough excuse. Careful to keep quiet despite Jerome's heavy breath, Martin bundled into warm waterproof gear. He grabbed a large trash bag and dug the half-frozen cardboard and packaged ingredients out of the snow with his gloved hands. Simple and satisfying work, something to focus on besides haunted thoughts.

Martin's cheeks felt the cold, but his hands stayed dry inside his gloves. The unprotected parts of his face felt good in contact with the unmoderated elements. A pleasant contrast with the heat inside his clothes. Bare face in contrast with his daily life behind barriers and masks. Out here, Martin's natural skin felt alive. It breathed, winced, numbed. His cheeks smarted when a gust of snow sprayed his face, a sensation like wet pins. Martin savored the exposure, savored the digging, savored the safety of the outdoors.

Done gathering the trash, he tied up the bag and walked it down the long driveway. He didn't rush. Little over a century ago, no person ventured near these woods without a weapon in hand. Early homesteaders shot the natural predators, believing they were a threat to communities and livestock. Later, as the human population grew, government regulations sentenced local wolves to extinction by mandating their slaughter. Bounty hunting laws required the eradication of wolves. Folktales of ravenous beasts preying upon innocents by night persisted long after the wolves were all gone.

The stories of monsters never scared him as a boy. For Martin, the woods were a safe space, the outdoors his real home. Martin knew about predators. The most dangerous beasts dwelled inside the house.

And now they were all gone, too.

Martin dropped the trash bag on the quiet roadside and held still, sensing the verdant landscape beneath the new snow. He avoided going back to the house. Martin looked up at the sky. More stars than he was used to seeing, and the moon was nearly full. Winter solstice: Bobby's favorite season to stalk. Martin looked up and down the empty road, and then pitched a low wolf-howl to the glowing moon. Silly, this childhood game, but he had to know if anyone was left. If Bobby was out there, hunting him, waiting for him, as promised. Martin held his breath and listened for an answering cry.

None came.

He walked back to his inheritance. The house was worth a fortune, a historical landmark. Martin must be reasonable. Selling was foolish. He must keep the house, keep his nightmares in check, and keep his marriage alive and well. Jerome didn't need to be poisoned by Martin's bad memories. After all, Bobby's persecution had lasted little more than a full year.

Martin couldn't hide from his mother's dark eyes when she returned from the hospital. She was a Verdun by birth. His father had been an outsider, never welcomed into the clan. His mother said it made Martin special, gave him versatility and strength. The word *inbred* was never spoken in the Verdun household. During his mother's absence, Martin invoked it silently, cowering under his peers. When she returned, she didn't question him about what happened. That wasn't her way. Without a word she moved out of the house with her only son and cut all ties with her family forever. Martin never saw Bobby again.

Face to face with the wolf-head on the door, Martin's calm eroded drop by drop. A trick of the winter moonlight made the hungry eyes glow. Breath from the nostrils warmed Martin's cheeks, heat seepage from the old construction's poor insulation. A shuffle, a sniff.

An anguished yowling from inside.

A human cry.

Jerome.

***

Martin vaulted across the threshold and into the kitchen. The yowling stifled in a series of gasps. Jerome hunched, panting, leaning on the open refrigerator in the dark, illuminated by the yellow pall of the fluorescent appliance light. Jerome cradled his stomach. Bare feet scuffed through mangled carry-out containers and remnants of food scraps scavenged from the trash. Smears of grease and broken china littered the floor. Jerome moaned like a soul calling up to Martin from the depths of hell: "I'm hungry."

Martin froze. Bells chimed from the basement.

Jerome's head whipped around. "Do you hear that?"

Martin stood outside of himself, listening to his own voice. He sounded like a robot spouting bad dialogue. "You're not well. I told you you'd get sick. What did I tell you? Go back to bed."

Jerome huddled over the audible growl emerging from his stomach. Louder, impossibly loud, like an animal roaring to get out. Half-standing, half-crawling, Jerome followed the siren song of the bells.

"Go back to bed. You're sick. Stop this."

Tracking the sinister chimes, Jerome circled the kitchen island, sniffed at windows, and scented the ringing sound of his quarry to the cellar door. It hung unlatched, an oblong slash of greater darkness from rising from below. Jerome slipped through the crack and disappeared.

The refrigerator swung closed and left Martin alone in the dark.

It was good to be a robot, good not to panic, good not to feel a sense of creeping, desperate horror at the torment Martin caused the person he loved. None of this was possible, anyway. Martin the robot tried to laugh mechanically at the whole absurd idea, but the sound strangled in his throat, releasing a shrill whine.

Jerome wasn't one of the bloodline. None of this made sense. And yet, tonight was indeed the night of a solstice. Bobby's favorite. All the necessary steps had taken place: the feeding, the concupiscence, the mating knot.

How had it happened with no wolf-skin?

Two solstices came and went during the months that Martin stayed in the house. He'd learned to hate the sensation of any wolf-skin, even his own after Bobby stole it. The night before his mother returned, Martin crept into Bobby's room where the older boy held Martin's cherished wolf-skin hostage. Trembling as Bobby slept, Martin snatched it back. He ran with his pelt deep into the woods; ran not as a wolf, but as a boy.

Under a thin canopy of spring buds, far inside the forest, Martin tore at the pelt with his fingers and teeth, trying to rend it. The skin resisted, strong and supple. He beat it with the sharp edges of rocks. No effect. He must destroy it, destroy this part of his body that made his body betray him. He'd stay human, invulnerable to Bobby, or to anyone else. Furious at the wolf-skin's resilience, Martin ground it into the dirt with his heel, spit on it, pissed on it, and said a makeshift curse over it. In the end, he dug a hole with his hands, and came home with ripped out fingernails and bloodied bare knuckles.

Jerome had no wolf-skin by birth. Now he ran unprepared in soft human form to be ripped apart below. There were pelts in the crypt, the skins of Martin's forebears. Jerome didn't share Martin's blood, but what if there was more to kinship than mere blood?

I didn't mean to do this.

Martin dreaded the sensation of a wolf-skin. Through ignorance or neglect, he'd forced Jerome into the ritual. He must now be like Bobby and force Jerome to share a wolf-skin with him to survive.

I can't. I love him.

Bobby's leer swam up at Martin through a blur of tears. Human eyes shrank into black slits. Teeth in the panting mouth multiplied and grew long and ragged. The breath of the wolf dried Martin's tears, though he barely realized he was crying. Warm saliva foamed on Bobby's quivering tongue.

If you love him, come and find him. Hide and seek. That's my good boy.

How Martin hated that voice.

It was time to hunt.

Martin forced his feet to follow the call of the bells. The thud of the cellar steps and smell of the smoke-tinged funerary air made Martin's senses scream at him to turn back. He passed through clean, refurbished corridors into older tunnels. Hard stone flooring gave way to pliant dirt. Ancient rafters bearing the weight of the earth closed around him, jointed at lower and lower angles until Martin had to walk on all fours. The walls seethed with hairy roots and smelled of dead leaves, an odor both rotten and robust. Energized, Martin loped. The heavy incense of the oven reached him through the darkness before he saw the fire's glow.

Emerging into a cavernous crypt, Martin recoiled. A confusion of scents oppressed him: acrid, savory, decayed, and sweet. Uninterred, a body lay on a slab near the oven. Elderly, recently deceased, with unmistakable Verdun features. Uncle Michel.

Three small, black-hooded figures worked around the corpse, mute except for the rattle and chime of bells beneath their cloaks. They were clothed exactly as the silent visitor from whom Martin had accepted the pastry box. They moved with similar hypnotic deliberation. One figure bowed beside a heap of roasted bones, grinding the fragments in an enormous stone mortar. A second mixed the resulting powdered bone meal with a rank liquid that slid instead of flowed when it was ladled out. The two took turns kneading the mixture into rounds of dough, and then pushed them into the oven with a blackened wooden paddle. A third figure, the largest of the three, pulled the finished funeral cakes from the oven, passed them over the corpse with ritualistic solemnity, and fed the small loaves to Jerome.

Martin rushed to Jerome and bundled his jacket into a cushion. Jerome whimpered and writhed on the dirt floor. Squeals and growls surged from inside Jerome's abdomen. Jerome moaned between feedings. Visible embryonic lumps bulged and squirmed beneath his open robe.

The figure closest to Jerome knelt with one of the unwholesome loaves, broke it in half, and emitted a hoarse, insistent whisper. "Thus the common meal is the pledge and witness of the unity of the kin, the means of repairing and renewing us. A new organism, a new domicile, a new clan. Country, kin and worship mingle in one unified body."

Though largest, the creature still lacked the stature of a human adult. It fingered something beneath its cloak while Jerome sated his hunger. Martin's attention went unwillingly to the creature's hand. It pulled an object from the folds of its garment. After a quivering pause, it held before Martin a grey and white furred pelt. It dangled just out of Martin's reach. A wolf-skin.

Yellow nails like overgrown teeth curled into the clean, lush fur. An odor familiar and fond in Martin's memory wafted from the skin. "I saved it for you. Say thank you, little pup."

Cold crept into Martin's chest.

Sharing the same blood was never enough for Bobby. He wanted to share the same skin. In the caverns of the cellar, Bobby had pounced. He'd bound Martin to him, clutched inside his own sickly pelt. Wrongly mated, Martin remained an un-transfigured boy, vulnerable to claws and teeth, helpless to hold back his human sobs. Bobby relinquished Martin's hostage wolf-skin only for whelping. No human body could survive, and Bobby wanted Martin alive.

The icy sensation in Martin's chest didn't paralyze him as in the past. His body stirred with cold, hard rage.

Martin lunged forward at the pelt. Bobby gripped the other end. Stretched between Martin and Bobby, the thick fur shone clean and the skin flexed without shredding. No trace of filth remained. Martin's wolf-skin had been groomed, brushed, and oiled for the past twenty years to maintain beauty, sheen, and elasticity. Bobby tugged on the edge of the wolf-skin to drag Martin closer. "I knew you'd come back to me."

"You tricked us."

"Us? A human isn't worthy of you. Say it to me."

"Not that. Not now."

"You used to say you loved me. Three times makes it a pact."

Martin twisted away from the creature's gaze, burning with shame, still gripping the wolf-skin. "I lied. I was trying to stay alive."

"Why won't you look me in the eye?"

Clasping the pelt with one white claw, Bobby pulled away his obscuring hood and cloak. He exposed the pale, taut hide of long-term starvation, the hairless pate of premature age, the yellow eyes of a diseased animal, and the blackened teeth of a necrophage. Bobby was a shrunken amalgam, neither man nor wolf. Rotten dog-breath warmed Martin's face as Bobby leaned closer.

"You can't lie to me. I know you better than you know yourself. I dug a hole inside you so you'd always need me."

Martin yanked the pelt. Bobby stumbled, held on tight, and fell to his knees. Martin's voice exploded over the misshapen hybrid supplicating below him. "I lied to you because

I hate you. You disgust me. You know nothing about me."

Bobby's hoarse wheedling grew more sickening, more urgent.

"You were always my special one. Remember the things I taught you, the wonders we planned to share? In old times, the shapeshifters were shaman. We spared humans by our grace and slaughtered them at our will. The church drove our ancestors underground with their lies. They called us monsters because we were more like gods than their little priests. You and I will be great magicians again, great healers. We are mighty in unity, mighty in love."

"You've healed nothing, no one."

"Have you forgotten your birthright? How I nurtured and trained you? I made you what you are today. I made you strong." Bobby inhaled the air around Martin, and his eyes narrowed. "I can still smell myself inside of you."

Martin aimed for the bony paw clutching the pelt and plunged his human teeth into its charnel flesh. Blood spewed, nails clattered, and Bobby snatched his claws off the pelt. Yowling, Bobby coddled and sucked his wound. Martin rolled to the dirt floor and wrapped Jerome against his chest inside the wolf-skin. Jerome thrashed harder, moaned louder, fought the feral change taking over his body as Martin sank into the warm affinity of the skin.

Martin's senses sharpened. His painful memories of cloying disgust gave way to more ancient, joyful thoughts.

Martin ran free in the forest. His wolf-skin was a natural part of him. Body, identity, and mind: it felt good. It felt right. Before the torments of Uncle Michel's house, before Bobby's attacks, Martin ran free under sunlight and moonlight. Every scent he unearthed told a new story. Martin wore his muscular haunches as proud badges of strength. He bared his powerful fangs in defiance of any hunter's false prowess. He flashed his eviscerating claws, chaotic weapons worthy of his innate wildness. *I'm a beast*, his last fully human thought.

Jerome struggled against the transfiguring skin. Martin held him hard against his chest.

I'm a beast, he said or thought, his voice a canine huff. *I'm a beast but not a monster.*

A wolf-skin can only be shared by a true mate. Martin felt Jerome's heart beating, the insistent pressure against his own chest. He felt their separate pulses cease to fluctuate, then synchronize, and then bond in an enduring rhythm. Jerome transformed. Fitful in the hermaphrodite wolf-form, Jerome howled. Turning and restless, unable to escape his sudden biology, possessed of a litter both ravenous and ravenously growing, Jerome settled and began birthing the pups.

Martin prowled a perimeter around Jerome, wary, vicious, ready to fight. Martin had never had a partner to defend him. He'd spent each solstice cowering, as one by one, his pups were taken. A disciple of obscure black arts, Bobby harvested his primitive sacraments from the litter. He ate his own while Martin watched.

The cloaked creatures loyal to Bobby circled Martin as he guarded Jerome. They drew Martin's snarls with feigned attacks, came from opposite directions, and taunted with bells and small knives. Martin spun, and Bobby snatched a live pup. He shoved the squealing infant into the black pit of his mouth. Martin pounced, and Bobby leapt twenty feet aloft and landed on the elderly Verdun corpse on the slab. Bobby's emaciated frame, pallid from a life underground, deprived of the joy of the hunt, and malnourished by the lack of healthy moonlight, arced like a swinging sickle over his father. He rocked back and forth, and then vomited the sacrificial offspring into the dead man's mouth.

Perched on the corpse, Bobby peeled away a sleeve of skin from his own chest, exposing gangrenous dead flesh. The pungent smell of decay was not lessened by the purifying flames that burned in the funerary oven. Numerous scars crosshatched Bobby's body. Healing had hardened his skin into a tight, articulated cage. Bobby stretched the lappet of torn skin across the corpse's heart.

The dead man sputtered. Bobby held his mouth shut. "Papa, keep it down."

Bobby forced his full weight into the task of feeding the dead man. Both claws crushed into the sunken face. Bobby's boney shoulders quivered with desperate effort. His breath came hoarse and fast. The corpse bucked: then it swallowed. The Verdun corpse shuddered and rolled onto its side. The sickly acolytes circled, enrapt. Bobby clung to his father, whispering incantations. Uncle Michel's corpse wheezed, taking in a long, involuntary breath.

Bobby's eyes remained fixed on his father. "We never die, by the pledge and witness of the unity of the kin."

Jerome snarled, revived from feasting on afterbirth. Like Martin, Jerome had a healthy canine frame, and a glorious, full pelt. His eyes were vibrant, his ears alert.

A wordless, instinctual exchange passed between Martin and Jerome: a glance condensed months of conversation. Betrayals, secrets, apologies; then forgiveness, the reconstruction of trust. They sensed the full spectrum of each other's emotions, shared fierce delight in their magical bodies and miraculous offspring. The newborn pups they must now protect.

Martin's lip twitched. Jerome rose and growled. Martin pointed his ears toward their prey and bared his teeth. They launched as one beast and then split, Jerome flying at the two cloaked figures and Martin at Bobby's throat.

Martin crushed Bobby under his fangs, grinding the gristle around Bobby's windpipe. He shredded the stringy muscles of Bobby's esophagus, popping open arteries and veins. Mucous from Bobby's black gullet mingled with his spurting blood. The raw stew of carnage poisoned Martin's pleasure in revenge, but he would not stop. He showed no mercy, didn't consider it, didn't care about the petty morals of his human self. Martin lashed his frenzied jaws back and forth until the limp puppet of squalling gore that slid between his teeth ripped in half.

Bobby was dead long before Martin flung the powerless, dripping remains into the oven. More dazed than triumphant, Martin backed away. It was easy to kill Bobby. A disappointment after years of fear and hate. Time that Martin would never get back. Martin panted with strange grief as the thing he'd allowed to define his life devoured itself in flames.

Grabbing at the burning body, the two other cloaked creatures singed their paws. Fire chased them. One creature seized the wooden paddle from the oven and swung it flaming at Martin. Jerome went for its wrist and threw it off balance. The paddle dropped and tangled in the hybrid's cloak. Fast flames from the oven lit the creature like a torch.

Smoke clouded the chamber. Dry beams supporting the crypt and fuel from brittle bodies of the stunted hybrids and their ancient kin fed the blaze. Uncle Michel's corpse convulsed and wheezed, waking on the slab, breathing, rising.

Martin and Jerome hoisted their pups in gentle, powerful jaws and fled through the catacomb tunnels. They ran away from the house and far into the forested hills. They ran free, until no scent of fire touched their senses, no ash fell upon their fur. They journeyed deep into the verdant glades to make a new home in the open, where no trail of smoke placed a finger over the mouth of the moon.

***

Todd slept through his alarm. He stayed up too late partying after his shift and spent the morning half-stoned, tossing in bed. Restless, he dreamed he heard sirens. By the time he got the car running and reached the Verdun place, the sun had dwindled. Todd smelled the scorched wreckage ahead before he saw the charred, collapsed hull of the mansion and its blasted woodland gardens.

Slipping under the caution tape around the perimeter, Todd searched the ashes for something interesting or valuable. He nudged the debris with his foot. He hoped the men were okay, figured he'd have heard if anyone got hurt in the fire. The big guy seemed nice.

A gleam caught Todd's eye.

The setting sun teased him. It made the object shine like an expensive piece of jewelry. When Todd picked it up, he saw it was nothing but an odd, jagged shard of bone. He almost tossed it, and then thought about his cool biology teacher who might know what kind of animal it came from. He wouldn't say where he found it. Todd hid the bone in his backpack and put it under his bed until Monday morning. That night, instead of sirens, Todd dreamed he heard the howling of wolves.

BIOGRAPHY

Joe Koch (he/they) writes literary horror and surrealist trash. Joe is a Shirley Jackson Award finalist and the author of *The Wingspan of Severed Hands*, *The Couvade*, and *Convulsive*. They've had over fifty short stories published in books and journals like Year's Best Hardcore Horror, The Big Book of Blasphemy, and Not All Monsters. Find Joe online at horrorsong.blog and on Twitter @horrorsong.

ADRIAN BALDWIN (COVER ARTIST)

Adrian is a Mancunian now living and working in Wales. Back in the 1990s, he wrote for various TV shows/personalities: Smith & Jones, Clive Anderson, Brian Conley, Paul McKenna, Hale & Pace, Rory Bremner (and a few others). Wooo, get him! Since then, he has written three screenplays—one of which received generous financial backing from the Film Agency for Wales. Then along came the global recession which kicked the UK Film industry in the nuts. What a bummer! Not to be outdone, he turned to novel writing—which had always been his real dream—and, in particular, a genre he feels is often overlooked; a genre he has always been a fan of: Dark Comedy (sometimes referred to as Horror's weird cousin). *Barnacle Brat* (a dark comedy for grown-ups), his first novel won Indie Novel of the Year 2016 award; his second novel *Stanley Mccloud Must Die!* (more dark comedy for grown-ups) published in 2016 and his third: *The Snowman And The Scarecrow* (another dark comedy for grown-ups) published in 2018. Adrian Baldwin has also written and published a number of dark comedy short stories. He designs book covers too—not just for his own books but for a growing number of publishers. For more information on the award-winning author, check out: https://adrianbaldwin.info/

DEMAIN PUBLISHING

To keep up to-date on all news DEMAIN (including future submission calls and releases) you can follow us in a number of ways:

BLOG:
www.demainpublishingblog.weebly.com

TWITTER:
@DemainPubUk

FACEBOOK PAGE:
Demain Publishing

INSTAGRAM:
demainpublishing

Printed in Great Britain
by Amazon